DISASTER SCIENCE

THE SCIENCE OF AN AVALANCHE

CAROL HAND

Published in the United States of America
by Cherry Lake Publishing
Ann Arbor, Michigan
www.cherrylakepublishing.com

Consultants: Jennifer Cole, Ph.D., Department of Earth and Planetary Sciences at Harvard University;
Marla Conn, ReadAbility, Inc.
Editorial direction: Red Line Editorial
Book production: Design Lab
Book design: Sleeping Bear Press

Photo Credits: Rafal Belzowski/iStockphoto, cover, 1; Ted S. Warren/AP Images, 5; Library of Congress, 6; Chris
Warham/Shutterstock Images, 8; Shutterstock Images, 11, 14, 23; Dar Yasin/AP Images, 17; Galyna Andrushko/
Shutterstock Images, 21; Corbis, 25; iStockphoto, 26; Jeff McIntosh/The Canadian Press/AP Images, 28

Library of Congress Cataloging-in-Publication Data
   Hand, Carol, 1945– author.
   The science of an avalanche / by Carol Hand.
      pages cm — (Disaster science Set 2)
   Includes bibliographical references and index.
   Audience: Grades 4 to 6
   ISBN 978-1-63362-484-9 (hardcover : alk. paper) — ISBN 978-1-63362-500-6 (pbk. : alk. paper) —
ISBN 978-1-63362-516-7 (pdf ebook) — ISBN 978-1-63362-532-7 (hosted ebook)
   1. Avalanches—Juvenile literature. I. Title. II. Series: 21st century skills library. Disaster science.

   QC929.A8H37 2015
   551.57'848—dc23   2015005521

Cherry Lake Publishing would like to acknowledge the work of
the Partnership for 21st Century Skills. Please visit www.p21.org
for more information.

Printed in the United States of America
Corporate Graphics
June 2015

ABOUT THE AUTHOR

Carol Hand is a science writer who specializes in earth and life sciences. She has a Ph.D. in zoology
and previously worked as a college teacher. She has written more than 25 books for young people,
including titles on glaciers, weather patterns, and climate.

TABLE OF CONTENTS

CHAPTER 1

Avalanche in the Cascade Mountains

In the early 1900s, the *Spokane Express* train brought passengers through the Cascade Mountains in Washington. Weather in the area could be harsh. In winter, heavy snowstorms often delayed trains for up to 24 hours. One snowstorm in February 1910 was much more destructive than the others. It led to the most devastating **avalanche** in US history.

In an area of the mountains called Stevens Pass, snow fell for more than a week. The snow piled 6 to 10 feet (1.8 to 3 m) high. Crews tried to clear the

Heavy snow is common in some mountainous areas of Washington.

railroad tracks, but they could not keep up with the heavy snowfall. The *Spokane Express* was stuck on the tracks, with dozens of passengers on board. A mail train was also stuck.

Officials sent the trains to side tracks to wait until crews could clear the main tracks. The side tracks were carved into a steep hillside, under overhanging snow. The trains stayed there for six days as the blizzard continued. Some people left the trains on foot. They hiked through deep drifts or slid down the snowy mountainside to the town. But some people thought this escape route was too dangerous, so they stayed on the train. Railway workers also stayed to assist passengers.

Eventually, the snow changed to rain. On the evening of February 28, a thunderstorm began. Late that night, a loud clap of thunder jolted people from sleep. They were met with disaster. A wall of snow half a mile (805 m)

Trains occasionally encountered avalanches during the early 1900s.

wide broke loose and crashed down the mountainside. The force of this avalanche pushed both trains into the nearby Tye River Gorge and buried them. Thirty-five passengers and 61 railroad workers died. About 23 people survived but had serious injuries. A frozen pocket watch in the wreckage had stopped at 1:42 a.m., the approximate time of the avalanche.

An avalanche is a mass of snow and ice that plunges down a mountainside or over a cliff. Its speed and force are so great that it can carry along earth, rocks, and even buildings in its path. Certain weather conditions can

In some countries, yellow and black flags warn people about avalanche risks.

lead to avalanches. In Stevens Pass, the snowstorm followed by rain helped cause the avalanche. The heavy **snowpack** on the mountainside became unstable, and a large piece of it broke off.

The Stevens Pass avalanche was deadly, but it made people more aware of the danger of avalanches. Some communities introduced safety measures to help people survive avalanches. Yet even today, these disasters kill approximately 150 people each year. Scientists are continuing to study how to improve avalanche safety.

THE AVALANCHE DISK

An exhibit at the Museum of Science and Industry in Chicago, Illinois, shows visitors an avalanche in motion. The Avalanche Disk demonstrates how ice and snow move. The disk is a circle tilted to mimic a mountain slope. It is 20 feet (6 m) across and contains white glass beads and red sand. The beads and sand represent particles, or small pieces, of ice and snow. The disk models the forces that act on these particles. Visitors can adjust the rotation of the disk. This shows how speeding up and slowing down the particles affects their motion.

The force of **gravity** constantly pulls down on the snow on a mountain slope. **Friction** and **cohesion** hold the snow together. Friction causes objects to slow down when they rub together. Cohesion causes particles to stick together. When gravity becomes stronger than friction and cohesion, an avalanche occurs.

What Causes an Avalanche?

Most avalanches occur high on mountain slopes. On some mountains, winter snow doesn't melt. New snow falls on top of old snow. The top layers compress and harden the deeper layers, forming a snowpack. Sometimes, parts of the snowpack break loose, triggering an avalanche.

Avalanches can be large or small. While some are very dangerous, others are too small or remote to cause much damage. Avalanches may contain only snow, ice, and air, but some also include rocks, trees, and chunks of other solid matter.

An avalanche occurs in the Italian Alps.

The most common natural cause of an avalanche is heavy snowfall. Heavy snow increases pressure on the snowpack. It can become unstable, causing sections to break off. When the bottom snow layers have turned to ice, new snow on top is more likely to slide off, forming an avalanche. Avalanches often occur in places with **wind slab**, which forms when wind forces large masses of snow to compact. These large masses of snow hang over the edge of a slope. Strong winds can cause wind slabs to collapse.

Humans can also cause avalanches. When people cut down trees on mountain slopes, they make the winter snowpack less stable. Activities that cause vibrations, such as using snowplows and snowmobiles, weaken the snowpack. The weight and movement of skiers can crack the snowpack and trigger an avalanche.

Scientists divide avalanches into four types: loose snow, wet snow, slab, and powder snow. A loose snow avalanche usually occurs after a snowfall, before the new snow has had time to pack down. It can start small and widen as it moves down the slope. A wet snow avalanche happens after rain falls in a snowy area. This kind of avalanche begins as a combination of water and snow. It travels slowly at first, collecting rocks and other debris, then quickly picks up speed.

In a slab avalanche, a large block of ice and snow breaks loose and tumbles down the slope of a mountain. The amount of damage depends on the size of the block. Often, people trigger slab avalanches. Skiers help cause them in places where unstable layers of snow cover a compressed bottom layer of snow. If several skiers are too

SLAB AVALANCHE

A slab avalanche occurs when pressure on a hard top layer of ice and snow causes cracks to form. A slab or block can break off, creating an avalanche.

slab of ice and snow

weak snow layer

compressed snow layer

A rescue helicopter searches for skiers trapped in an avalanche.

close together when they go down the slope, the extra weight may crack the ice or snow on top. The crack continues along the skiers' path, triggering an avalanche.

A powder snow avalanche combines a slab avalanche and a loose snow avalanche. A large chunk of ice breaks off, and a mass of powdered snow follows it down. The powder can form snowballs as it travels, increasing the size of the avalanche. Powder snow avalanches are very dangerous. They can travel up to 190 miles per hour (306 kmh) and cover large distances.

How Science Works
PING-PONG PREDICTORS

To learn more about avalanches, Japanese scientists dropped hundreds of thousands of ping-pong balls down a ski slope. Studying their fall showed the scientists what might happen during a powder snow avalanche. The scientists hope their observations can help them predict where an avalanche might go. As a result, they may be able to help people survive and respond to avalanches.

Ping-pong balls are very light. A mass of them moves down a slope in the same way a large mass of powdered snow moves. The ping-pong balls are easier to study than real snow. They are larger and easier to see. Scientists know the number and weight of the balls. They can use them to test a hypothesis about where an avalanche will go. If the hypothesis is true for the ping-pong balls, it will probably be true for an actual avalanche.

Loose snow avalanches are the most common type of avalanche. Slab avalanches and powder snow avalanches cause the most deaths and injuries. However, any type of avalanche can be dangerous.

CHAPTER 3

What Happens in an Avalanche?

Scientists cannot predict exactly when an avalanche will happen. But they can identify times and places where avalanches are likely to occur. Often, there are warning signs before an avalanche begins.

One risk factor is recent avalanche activity. In a place where an avalanche has recently happened, the snowpack is often still unstable. Another warning sign is rising temperatures. In a snowy area, warmer temperatures cause snow to begin melting. The snow then slides more easily. For this reason, avalanches often

Tourists walk in a part of northern India known for avalanches.

happen in late winter and early spring. A third sign that an avalanche might be likely is a snowfall within the past 24 hours. Snow is more likely to slide when it has little time to compact. Spring or summer rainfall can also weaken the snowpack in mountainous areas, triggering avalanches.

An avalanche has three main parts. The **starting zone** is the least stable part of the slope, where snow is most likely to break off and fall. It is usually, but not always, near the top. The **avalanche track** is the path

Caught in an Avalanche

In 1978, Bruce Tremper was skiing in Montana when he got caught in an avalanche. Tremper compared the experience to being "stuck in a giant washing machine filled with snow." Grabbing a tree helped protect him, but the tree eventually broke. Tremper tumbled down the slope. When he stopped, heavy snow had buried him to his waist. Today, Tremper talks to skiers about his experience to help them prepare for avalanches.

the avalanche takes as it moves down the slope. A narrow path where all the trees are missing might indicate a past avalanche. The **runout zone** is the region at the bottom where the avalanche stops, and snow and debris pile up.

A naturally caused mountain avalanche might release as much as 300,000 cubic yards (230,000 m³) of snow. Avalanches triggered by skiers are typically smaller but may be more deadly, since there are usually more people nearby.

Large avalanches can bury towns. They can block highways and destroy buildings and power lines. The damage is greater if the avalanche carries rocks, trees, or other debris. Melting snow after an avalanche can cause flooding in low-lying areas. The floods may cause crop damage and power failures. Even if avalanches last a very short time, they can be devastating. Within seconds, avalanches can reach speeds of 70 to 80 miles per hour (110 to 130 kmh).

PARTS OF AN AVALANCHE

There are three main parts of an avalanche. At the starting zone, snow breaks away from the surrounding area and starts to slide. The track is the path of the avalanche as it moves. The avalanche stops at the runout zone, where the snow and ice pile up.

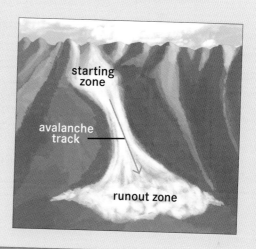

AVALANCHES AND CLIMATE

Many avalanches happen when temperatures increase and snow begins to melt. In recent years, scientists have begun to study the effects of a changing climate on avalanches.

Between 1880 and 2012, the average world temperature increased by 1.53 degrees Fahrenheit (0.85°C). But temperatures in the Himalaya Mountains, also known as the Himalayas, in Asia are warming three times faster. The warming temperatures in this region cause ice to melt and glaciers to collapse. Many scientists

An avalanche occurs in the Himalaya Mountains.

say these conditions could cause a rise in avalanches. In April 2014, a massive avalanche on Mount Everest, the world's tallest mountain, killed 16 native Sherpa guides. In October of that same year, a blizzard and avalanche in the Himalayas killed 39 more people.

As glaciers thaw, they become less stable. It is difficult to predict when they might crack and collapse. Scientists have been using satellites to study Himalayan glaciers for only the last 10 years. They are not certain how weather conditions in the mountains will change in the future.

Avalanche Rescue Dogs

Searching for people buried under snow is dangerous. After an avalanche, snow in the area is still unstable. If rescue workers walk on it, they can trigger another disaster. In the French Alps, trained dogs help find avalanche survivors. The dogs are lightweight. They can walk quickly across unstable snow without breaking through. Their sense of smell allows them to locate people buried in snow and alert a rescue team.

A similar situation is occurring in the European Alps. Average Alpine temperatures are rising twice as fast as average global temperatures. As a result, mountain slopes are becoming less stable. The base layer of Alpine snow is typically thin, weak, and icy. New snow does not stick well to it, making avalanches likely.

Often, people think only heavy snow causes avalanches. Yet less snowfall may also be dangerous. In recent years, many parts of the world have had less snowfall than in the past. In addition, much of it has been "sugary snow" that does not stick together well. This kind of snow forms a thin, unstable snowpack. The thin layers change shape and weaken over time. When new snow falls, people can easily disturb weak snow layers and trigger an avalanche.

Trainers work with avalanche rescue dogs in Europe.

AVALANCHE SAFETY AND PREVENTION

People in areas where avalanches occur take safety seriously. Town and city planners keep careful records of the sizes and locations of avalanches. The planners use these records to determine the types of structures to build and where to build them safely.

One way to prevent or control avalanches is by creating small avalanches when no one is on the slopes. Researchers use explosives to trigger avalanches in remote areas. By creating small, controlled avalanches after a heavy snow, they clear some of the snowfall off

[21ST CENTURY SKILLS LIBRARY]

In the 1960s, park rangers used special rifles to shoot down snow on high slopes.

high slopes. This may prevent larger avalanches. Sometimes, researchers use **ski checking** to test the stability of the snow. In a ski check, an expert skier deliberately skis across cracks in the snow. Ski checking requires a partner who can rescue the skier if he or she triggers an avalanche.

People can set up barriers to change an avalanche path or stop the snow as it slides down. In the United States and Canada, avalanches are likelier to occur in places where forests were cut down. People are now

In Tyrol, Austria, barriers help protect people from avalanches.

planting new trees in some of these areas. Trees provide natural barriers that lower the risk of avalanches.

In mountainous parts of Europe, some people build permanent structures for protection. They construct steel snow bridges and flexible snow nets made of steel cables. These structures protect roads and settlements by forming barriers that block falling snow.

In the avalanche path and runout zone, dams can stop snow or change its path. The dams can be up to 66 feet (20 m) deep. Some towns build sheds or tunnels over roads. Snow piles on top of them, allowing cars to travel safely. People also work to protect individual homes. Reinforced walls around houses can break up an avalanche.

Skiers and snowboarders can sometimes prevent avalanches by avoiding the slopes during risky times. This means learning about dangerous weather conditions before going onto the snow. Every skier on a snowpack should have survival gear and companions.

People can survive some avalanches. Survivors typically get out before an avalanche stops or do not become

PREVENTING AVALANCHE DEATHS IN SWITZERLAND

In the winter of 1951, avalanches in the Swiss Alps caused 98 deaths. Officials and homeowners responded by building many protective structures. In the winter of 1999, a similar number of avalanches happened. This time, the avalanches caused only 17 deaths. The structures helped protect people from danger.

A rescue team in Canada searched for survivors after an avalanche in 2008.

completely buried. Skiers caught in an avalanche should try to get out as soon as they can. Grabbing onto trees can help. People who become buried in snow should make swimming motions to stay near the surface. They should stay calm as they wait for rescue.

In recent years, people have learned warning signs of avalanches. New safety measures have helped save lives. Yet avalanches can still have devastating effects. Research teams, communities, and individuals must continue to take steps to prevent and avoid avalanches.

[21ST CENTURY SKILLS LIBRARY]

PREDICTING AVALANCHES BY UNDERSTANDING SNOW

In a "cold lab" at Montana State University, Ed Adams and other scientists study how snow moves under different circumstances. Using computer models, they **replicate** possible weather conditions on a snowy mountain. They control factors such as temperature, sunlight, slope, and types of snow. By replicating these conditions and testing them many times, the scientists learn how snow moves in different types of weather. The models help them predict situations that will cause an avalanche.

Adams says that it is necessary to understand snow layers in order to understand avalanches. A weak layer covered by a solid layer is most likely to trigger an avalanche. Weak layers are made of very smooth snow crystals that do not stick together. In strong layers, crystals bond to each other. The surface layer is key to forecasting avalanches. Sun and cold at the surface cause snow crystals to change. In the cold lab, Adams and the other scientists study how these changes happen.

TOP FIVE WORST AVALANCHE EVENTS

1. **Yungay, Peru, May 31, 1970**
   An offshore earthquake triggered an avalanche on Mount Huascaran in the Andes Mountains. The avalanche buried the town of Yungay, killing at least 18,000 people.

2. **Dolomites, Italy, December 1916**
   During World War I (1914–1918), Austrian troops set up camp under a mountain with unstable snow where avalanches occurred. Over several weeks, approximately 10,000 soldiers died in the avalanches. Austrians called the worst day of the avalanches White Friday.

3. **Ranrahirca, Peru, January 10, 1962**
   A block of ice from a glacier slid down Mount Huascaran, creating an avalanche that destroyed nine towns and seven villages. Historians estimate that 2,700 to 4,000 people died in the disaster.

4. **Plurs, Switzerland, September 4, 1618**
   An avalanche that began in the village of Rodi buried the nearby town of Plurs. The death toll was 2,427. Only four residents of Plurs, who were traveling at the time, survived.

5. **Swiss-Austrian Alps, Winter 1950–1951**
   This winter became known as the Winter of Terror, as high precipitation levels led to almost 650 avalanches. They hit many towns and killed more than 265 people.

LEARN MORE

FURTHER READING

Garbe, Suzanne. *The Worst Avalanches of All Time*. Mankato, MN: Capstone, 2012.

Shone, Rob. *Avalanches and Landslides*. New York: Rosen, 2014.

Spilsbury, Richard. *The Science of Avalanches*. New York: Gareth Stevens, 2013.

Woods, Michael, and Mary B. Woods. *Disasters Up Close: Avalanches*. Minneapolis: Lerner, 2007.

WEB SITES

National Avalanche Center: Get the Training
www.fsavalanche.org/get-the-training
This Web site explains how to recognize avalanche warning signs.

National Geographic: Unleash an Avalanche
environment.nationalgeographic.com/environment/natural-disasters/avalanche-interactive
This Web site provides activities and interactive models of avalanches.

GLOSSARY

avalanche (AV-uh-lanch) a mass of snow and ice moving rapidly down a mountainside or over a cliff

avalanche track (AV-uh-lanch trak) the path taken by an avalanche as it moves down a slope

cohesion (co-HEE-zhun) the act or state of sticking together tightly

friction (FRIK-shun) the force that causes an object to slow down when it rubs against another object

gravity (GRAV-uh-tee) the force that causes objects to fall toward the center of Earth

replicate (REP-li-kayt) copy exactly, especially in an experiment

runout zone (RUN-out zohn) region at the base of an avalanche where snow and debris stop and pile up

ski checking (SKEE chek-ing) skiing across a crack in the snowpack to determine the likelihood of an avalanche

snowpack (SNO-pak) a mass of snow that is compressed and hardened by its own weight

starting zone (START-ing zohn) the beginning part of an avalanche, where the snowpack is unstable and most likely to break

wind slab (WIND slab) a slab of snow that forms when wind drives together and compacts large amounts of snow

INDEX

32

[21ST CENTURY SKILLS LIBRARY]